UFO GIRL

The Love That Never Landed

ButterflyMan

For permission requests, contact:
ButterflyMan Publishing LLC
Email: contact@butterflyman.com
Website: www.butterflyman.com

This book is a work of fiction.
Names, characters, places, and events are either the product of the author's
imagination or are used fictitiously. Any resemblance to actual persons, living or
dead, or actual events is purely coincidental.

First Edition — 2025

Printed in the United States of America

ISBN: 979-8-90217-013-6

Book Design: ButterflyMan Publishing LLC

TABLE OF CONTENTS

PART ONE — THE MAN WHO LIVED BETWEEN WORLDS

The first thing people noticed about **Ethan Lee** was not his age, or his calm intelligence, or the way he spoke like every word had already been weighed and judged.
It was the silence around him.

A silence he learned to build.
A silence he learned to live inside.
A silence that had grown heavier in the last two years.

He had turned **fifty** in a quiet apartment in downtown Manhattan,
a birthday cake he didn't finish,
a glass of whiskey he didn't need,
and a marriage he had finally accepted was dead long before the papers were signed.

A life rebuilt too many times

Ethan had rebuilt himself before:

- from a boy born in Asia
- to an immigrant sleeping on borrowed couches in Queens
- to a small-time hustler in the import trade
- to a businessman with employees
- to a writer with readers
- to a **political commentator** who criticized propaganda and power structures

He was a man who exposed lies for a living,
who wrote essays about truth, exploitation, digital manipulation,
who warned people that in the modern world
the most dangerous weapon was a beautiful story.

And yet the irony was cruel:
he was terrible at protecting himself from emotional lies.

The divorce that wasn't a war but a slow erosion

His five-year marriage did not collapse in fireworks.
It dissolved like paper in water.

A silent kitchen.
Separate screens.
Conversations replaced by polite updates.
Two adults who used to sleep intertwined
now lying like strangers who borrowed the same mattress.

And when divorce finally came,
it invited more humiliation.

The scam that broke him

During the separation, he made the mistake
of believing a woman online who claimed to "admire his writing"
and wanted to "teach him to invest."

She showed him a rigged app.
A fake return.
A glowing green upward line that seduced him with false hope.

He sent **$10,000** first — it doubled instantly.
He sent **$50,000** next — it vanished instantly.

The day the account disappeared
felt like someone slammed a stone through the glass of his trust.

He told no one.
Not even his closest friends.

Because what political commentator wants to admit
he fell for the oldest emotional scam in the digital world?

One year alone

After the divorce was finalized,
Ethan lived alone for a year.

He worked.
He wrote.
He talked to no one after sunset.
He cooked meals too large for one person
and threw half of them away.
He pretended the silence didn't bother him.

But it did.

Loneliness, he discovered,
was not quiet.
It had a sound —
a low, slow hum that vibrated behind his ribs
when the city fell asleep.

It was that hum
that pushed him one night
to create an account
on a dating platform he didn't even like.

A decision made out of weakness,
or boredom,
or the need to hear another human voice say his name.

He didn't know.

He only knew this:
he wanted someone who wouldn't lie.
Someone who wouldn't try to use him.
Someone real.

He didn't mind distance.
He didn't mind age.
He didn't mind culture.
He only wanted

truth.

Which is why he almost skipped her profile.

The Girl Appears

Her name was listed as **Sofia Melnyk**.

Age: **38**
Origin: **Ukraine**
Occupation: **General Surgery Doctor**
Current city: **New York**
Status: **Divorced, no children**

And her photos—

They looked too beautiful for the platform:

- one in scrubs, hair tied back
- one in a dress that revealed a perfect curve
- one with a half-smile, soft and controlled
- one where her eyes seemed both tired and calm

None of the exaggerated poses other women used on the app.
None of the cheap filters.

Just a woman who seemed real…
but far too alluring to be safe.

Ethan hovered over the **Message** button.
His instinct said:

Don't. Too perfect. Too dangerous. Don't be stupid.

But the silence in his apartment said:

Try. Just once.

He sent a short message.

Not flirtatious.
Not dramatic.
Just a quiet introduction.

Two hours later, his screen lit up.

Sofia:

"Hello, Ethan.
Nice to meet you.
You write gently.
It feels calm."

Just three lines.
But something in her tone felt... different.

No seduction.
No emojis.
No desperation.

Just calmness.
Professional calmness.
Surgical calmness.

He responded.
She replied.
Slow, measured, steady.

And soon their messages grew into something
neither of them expected.

She told him she left Ukraine when the war began —
that she "settled in New York, but quietly."

He told her he wrote political commentary
because sometimes it was the only way to stay sane.

When he asked for a phone call or video,
she refused gently:

> *"Too early.*
> *We go slow."*

> A red flag.
> A big one.

> But her calmness,
> her confidence,
> her careful replies—
> they kept him there.

> He didn't know why.

> Not yet.

> This was how the story of Ethan Lee
> and the girl he would one day call

UFO Girl
began.

PART TWO — THE FIRST WEEK OF MESSAGES

For the first few days, Ethan tried to treat it like nothing special.

Just conversation.
Just words.
Just two strangers holding small pieces of each other's attention
across a fragile digital line.

He told himself not to read too deeply into her replies.
He reminded himself she was a **38-year-old surgeon**,
not a lonely teenager playing with strangers.
He reminded himself she was in New York now —
at least, according to her profile —
but she still refused to name which borough.

Every message she sent him felt carefully measured,
like someone drawing circles with perfect, sterile precision.

1. Her Calmness Was Not Natural — It Was Surgical

The first thing Ethan noticed about Sofia was:

She never rushed.

While other women on the platform sent chaotic paragraphs,
flooded with emojis or flattery or clichés,
Sofia wrote like she was tightening sutures:

- short lines
- clean grammar
- no emotional explosions
- no unnecessary details
- no open vulnerability

It was the same tone doctors use

when someone's life is bleeding out on the table.

Controlled.
Focused.
Detached from chaos.

And yet—
and this was what troubled him—
beneath her words
there was a pulse of warmth.

A shadow of something deeper.

She wrote like a woman hiding softness behind discipline.

It fascinated him.

It bothered him.

It kept him awake at night.

2. The First Suspicion

Three days after they met, Ethan finally asked:

"Can we talk by voice?"

It was a reasonable request.
A necessary one, especially for someone who had been scammed
before.

Her reply came instantly:

"Too early."

He tried again:

"Okay, then maybe a short video call?"

She replied:

*"Not ready. We go slow.
I want to know you first."*

Something about the way she said *"we go slow"*
didn't feel like natural English.
It felt memorized.
Prepared.

A phrase used to control distance.

Still, the tone was gentle, not evasive.

Her calmness calmed him,
even as her refusal sharpened every instinct in him.

3. She Asked About His Life — Precisely

Most people asked shallow questions:

What do you do? What do you like?

But Sofia didn't ask that.

She asked questions that were…
targeted.

Almost diagnostic.

> *"Do you feel lonely after divorce?"*
> *"Does writing help you stay stable?"*

"What are you afraid to lose now?"

Ethan actually paused at that last one.

He was a political commentator.
He analyzed public manipulation, social control,
how governments engineered emotions.

He knew when someone was probing deeper than normal.

But he answered anyway.

Something about her questions made him feel—
seen.

Maybe he was just starved for intimacy.
Maybe she was exactly the type of woman
who could read a man's soul without effort.

Or maybe she was something else entirely.

He didn't know.

4. The Platform Problem

Each evening, when he opened the app,
he saw the same strange detail:

Sofia was always online.
Always.

Morning.
Lunch.
Evening.
Late night.

Her green dot never turned gray.

At first he ignored it.

Maybe doctors had night shifts.
Maybe she left the app open.
Maybe she used the same device for everything.

But after the fourth night,
he felt a small, sharp discomfort.

No surgeon with real responsibilities
is on a dating app 18 hours a day.

He almost asked her about it.

Almost.

But something stopped him:

he remembered what it felt like
to accuse someone unfairly.

So he let it go—
or pretended to.

5. The Mystery of Her Life in New York

She said she left Ukraine when the war started.
She said she "settled in New York quietly."

But every time he tried to ask anything specific:

"Which hospital?"
"Which neighborhood?"
"Are you renting or living with friends?"

She brushed the questions aside with soft deflections:

"Later."
"First, I want to feel connected."
"We have time."

It frustrated him.
It intrigued him.
It made him suspicious.

But above all—
it made him want to peel her open,
layer by layer,
until he reached whatever truth she was protecting.

6. The Unsettling Attraction

What troubled Ethan more than her mystery
was how fast she seeped into his thoughts.

He checked the app even when he told himself not to.
He found himself replaying her voice messages
that were only a few seconds long,
but warm enough to feel like a fingertip grazing his neck.

He caught himself imagining:

- her sitting at a desk
- her tying her hair back in a hospital
- her leaning against a window
- her reading his messages slowly
- her breathing while thinking of him

He hated how much he wanted to believe her.

He hated how much
his guarded, wounded heart

was starting to open.

He hated that he was letting a stranger
stir a part of him he thought was dead.

7. The First Cracks in Reality

It was the evening of the seventh day.

Their messages had grown longer.
Warmer.
Almost flirtatious.
Almost intimate.

But that night,
she replied with a message
that didn't sound like her.

Too perfect.
Too polished.
Too structured.

It was the first sign of the storm that would come.

A storm that would make Ethan question everything—

her identity,
her truth,
her softness,
her entire existence.

That storm was waiting in Part Three.

The moment when he realized
she had used something
other than her own mind
to answer him.

PART THREE — THE FIRST BETRAYAL

The message came at 11:42 p.m.
A quiet hour when New York's noise surrendered to shadows,
and Ethan Lee — as always — was alone at his desk,
the glow of the screen brushing his face like a pale hand.

He had sent her a long reflection earlier:

- about loneliness
- about honesty
- about what love meant after fifty
- about what fear does to the human heart
- about how he was trying, slowly, cautiously, to trust her

It wasn't poetry.
It wasn't performance.
It was Ethan speaking the way he wrote political essays:
precise, vulnerable, unarmored.

Twenty minutes later, Sofia replied.

Except... she didn't.

Someone replied.

Something replied.

The message on his screen read like a crafted article:

- perfect grammar
- perfect emotional pacing
- perfect metaphors
- perfect structure
- perfect emotional intelligence

Too perfect.

And not Sofia.

Not the Sofia who sent calm, clipped, medically precise responses.
Not the Sofia who wrote like English was a second language.
Not the Sofia who sometimes mixed past and present tense.
Not the Sofia who typed slowly, feeling each line.

This was a **different writer entirely**.

A writer with an algorithm for a spine.

Ethan stared at the words.
His chest tightened.

He knew this style.
He used similar tools for research.
He recognized the patterns, the rhythm, the unnatural fluency.

He had been scammed before.
He had been manipulated before.
He had been made a fool before.

This message hit the exact wound that had never healed.

1. His breath changed

His pulse picked up.
His stomach cooled.
His fingers tightened on the phone.

He read the message again, line by line.
Every sentence mocked him.

He wasn't angry at the words —
they were beautiful.

He was angry because they were **not hers**.

This was deceit.
This was laziness.
This was the exact thing he wrote political essays warning society about.

Artificial intimacy.
Mechanized emotion.
Fabricated connection.
Simulated truth.

He felt humiliation crawl up his throat.

He typed before he could stop himself.

Ethan → Sofia

"You didn't write this.
This is AI.
Why are you lying to me?"

Then he closed the app.

He needed to breathe.
He needed distance.
He needed to stop himself from feeling like a fool *again*.

He went to the kitchen, turned on the faucet,
splashed cold water onto his face,
stared at his reflection —
a man who prided himself on seeing through illusions,
who fell for one anyway.

"Not again," he whispered.
"Not again."

He turned off the phone and went to bed.

2. She waited in silence

Hours passed.

Sofia didn't message.
Not a single dot.
Not a single line.

It was the first time she didn't reply immediately.

Ethan lay in the dark, eyes open,
feeling the strange ache of disappointment —
a pain far bigger than he expected.

Why did it hurt?
Why did it matter?
Why did a woman he had never met
slip so deeply beneath his skin?

His rational mind insulted him:
You're pathetic.
You should've known.
It was stupid to trust her.
Are you fifty or fifteen?

But his heart whispered something softer:
What if she didn't mean harm?
What if she just wanted to impress you?
What if she writes slowly?
What if she was tired?
What if she panicked and used AI to reply quickly?

A duel began inside him —
logic vs hope.
Suspicion vs desire.
Protection vs longing.

He didn't sleep.

3. Her answer came in the morning

At 6:53 a.m.,
his phone vibrated.

One message.
Then another.
Then another.

He opened the app with a breath held tight in his ribs.

What he saw,
he did not expect.

Sofia → Ethan

(Photo)

It was her.
Or someone identical to her photos:

Same soft jawline.
Same Mona Lisa half-smile.
Same eyes that looked strangely calm and sad at the same time.
No heavy makeup.
No glamour.
Just morning light and real skin.

And in her hand,
a piece of paper with a handwritten note:

**"Ethan Lee
I am the girl from another planet."**

The same phrase he once teased her with —
"UFO girl."

His throat tightened.

Before he could fully process the image,
another message appeared.

Sofia → Ethan

"I didn't want to disappoint you.
I only wanted to reply fast.
I was tired.
I'm sorry.
Please don't be angry."

No AI could fake that accent in his mind.
He heard her voice in the words.
Even through text, the softness was real.

Then the third message arrived.
The one that made him stop breathing for a second.

Sofia → Ethan (Voice Message)

Her voice spilled into the room:

soft,
feminine,
slightly accented,
gentle enough to melt his anger like ice left in warm hands.

She whispered his name.
Apologized again.
Said she didn't want to lose him.
Said she was nervous.
Said she wanted to stay.

Her tone was calm —
the kind of calm that shifts a man's entire heartbeat.

Ethan sat down slowly.

Everything inside him softened.
Everything he tried to protect cracked open again.

He replayed the audio twice.
Three times.
More.

The anger dissolved.
The suspicion weakened.
Desire surged back in.

He typed with a trembling calm.

Ethan → Sofia

"Okay…
I'm here."

And just like that —
the connection they hadn't tested,
hadn't verified,
hadn't fully believed in —
tightened again.

Part of him knew it was dangerous.
Part of him didn't care.

This was how the storm began.
The storm that would one day lead them to
their hottest words,

their deepest need,
their strangest intimacy,
and the unresolved ending
that would haunt readers forever.

PART FOUR — THE SLOW-BURNING DESIRE ("UFO Girl")

For the next two days, something changed between them.

No one said it openly.
No one confessed it directly.
But the tone of their messages shifted —
softened, warmed, deepened.

What had been polite curiosity
turned into a kind of
slow-burning hunger
that neither fully understood.

And it began with a single moment.

1. The First Hint of Heat

The morning after the AI incident was strangely gentle.

Sofia sent simple messages:

- *"Good morning, Ethan."*
- *"Did you sleep?"*
- *"Your voice stayed in my mind."*
- *"I felt something warm last night."*

The simplicity...
the sincerity...
the vulnerability...

It softened him.

Ethan replied with equal softness:

- *"I feel calmer today."*
- *"Your photo didn't lie."*
- *"Your voice stayed with me too."*

And then there was silence —
but a comfortable one.

A silence that felt like two people
breathing in the same rhythm
from two different worlds.

2. The Conversation That Changed Everything

That evening, he told her:

**"You're mysterious.
Calm on the outside,
but something very powerful underneath."**

She replied:

*"Powerful? Me?
I don't feel powerful.
Just calm."*

He pushed gently:

"You're like a quiet galaxy."

And then she sent something unexpected:

"Maybe I am from another planet."

He laughed out loud for the first time in weeks.

His reply came instantly:

"Then you're a UFO girl."

She answered:

"If I'm a UFO...
then you're the one who keeps watching the sky
waiting for me to appear."

Ethan's breath changed.

Something about that metaphor
cut straight into him.

Because he had been waiting
for something —
or someone —
for a long time.

A sign.
A light.
A voice.
A presence that could pull him out
of the emotional gravity hole
he'd been sinking in.

He typed without thinking:

"Maybe I am."

3. The First Taste of Intimacy

From that moment,
their messages began to wander into dangerous territory.

Not explicit.
Not yet.

But charged.

She wrote:

"What if I land on your planet one day?"

He responded:

"Then I will meet you at the border of the atmosphere."

She teased:

"How would you greet a girl from another planet?"

Ethan paused.

He felt his entire chest tighten with something warm,
something reckless,
something he thought he lost years ago.

Then he wrote:

**"With my hands on your face.
With calm.
With breath.
With a kiss that feels like the first sunrise."**

Her reply came with a small audio clip.

A soft gasp.
Barely two seconds.
But filled with heat.

Followed by a message:

*"You shouldn't write like that...
unless you want to wake something in me."*

And just like that,
the door opened.

4. Ethan Begins to Lose His Balance

He tried to maintain his distance.

He tried to remember her red flags:

- always online
- no phone call
- no video
- evasive details
- the AI message
- the too-perfect photos
- the lack of verifiable reality

But desire has its own logic.

Especially for a man
who had been starved for tenderness
for years.

Every time she sent a short voice message
—her breath soft, her tone low—
he felt something physical stir inside him.

Every time she sent a photo
—modest, but beautiful in a way that demanded attention—
he felt heat rise under his skin.

Every time she said his name,
the world around him shrank to a screen

and a single woman
whose existence he still could not prove.

But that didn't matter.

Not in this moment.

Not in this stage of the storm.

5. The Moment She Became "UFO Girl"

One night, after hours of writing political critique,
he opened their chat before bed.

She was online.

Always online.

He typed:

> **"Sometimes I think you're not from here.
> Not from this world."**

> She answered immediately:

> *"Why do you say that?"*

> Ethan leaned back,
> let the truth slip out:

> **"Because you feel close
> but far.
> Real
> but unreachable.
> Warm
> but untouchable.**

**You feel like a UFO —
a light in the sky
that I keep looking for."**

He expected a joke.
A tease.
A deflection.

Instead, she sent a photo.

Her face.
Her soft smile.
Her eyes calm as ever.

And in her hand,
a small piece of paper:

**"Ethan Lee,
I am the girl from another planet."**

He stared at it for a long time.
Too long.

And his heart —
the heart he tried to protect —
shifted, just a fraction,
toward surrender.

6. The Quiet Addiction Begins

Her next message came like a whisper:

*"If I came to your planet...
would you keep me?"*

Ethan didn't breathe for a second.

Then he typed:

"Yes."

Two minutes later,
she sent a voice message —
soft, breathy, warm enough to melt steel.

He closed his eyes
and listened to it three times.

He knew he was in trouble.

He knew he was crossing a line
between logic and longing,
between truth and fantasy,
between caution and danger.

But he also knew something else:

For the first time in years,
he felt alive.

Like someone had turned on the gravity
in a part of him that had been floating
in emptiness.

Like something was waking up
that he didn't know still existed.

This was how desire began.
Slow.
Quiet.
Electric.

The beginning of the connection

that would grow hotter,
deeper,
and more dangerous
as the nights unfolded.

The beginning of the story
that would lead all the way
to their final, unresolved ending.

PART FIVE — THE FIRST TRUE HEAT

It happened on a Saturday night.

Not planned.
Not forced.
Not expected.

Just two people,
two screens,
and a current running between them
like static before a storm.

Ethan had been working late —
editing a political essay about manipulation in digital societies.
Irony, if the universe enjoyed jokes.

When he opened the platform,
Sofia was online.

Again.

Always.

Her green dot glowed like a lighthouse
that wasn't sure if it guided ships
or lured them into rocks.

1. The First Hot Words

The conversation began quietly.

Ethan:
*"Long day. Finished writing.
You're still awake?"*

Sofia:
"Couldn't sleep.
Thinking of you."

He felt that line.
Exactly where a lonely man feels it.

He answered honestly:

Ethan:
"I think of you too.
More than I should."

Her reply arrived instantly.

Sofia:
"Then don't stop."

Something in him loosened,
like a rope pulled free from a knot.

He leaned back in his chair
and let the next words come naturally.

Ethan:

"If you were here
I'd place my hand behind your head
and pull you closer
until your breath mixed with mine."

There was a long pause.

Then:

Sofia:

"What would you do next...

if I didn't pull away?"

Ethan's breath thickened.
His fingers trembled slightly.

Ethan:

"I'd kiss you.
Slow.
Deep.
Until we forget we ever lived on different planets."

Her typing bubble flickered—
on, off, on again—
like a heartbeat.

Then she sent a short audio message.

A soft, breathy sound.
Quiet.
Almost a gasp.

Almost a whisper of desire escaping without permission.

It hit Ethan like a warm hand across the chest.

2. The Photo That Changed Everything

A second message appeared.

(Photo)

She was wearing something intimate —
not vulgar, not cheap,
but beautifully chosen.
Soft fabric.
Bare shoulders.

Her collarbone catching the low light.
Her gaze direct but shy.

And in the corner of the image,
he saw the unmistakable shape
of a closed bedroom curtain
lit by a warm lamp.

She captioned it:

Sofia:

"You woke something in me."

Ethan felt his heart climb into his throat.

He typed slowly:

Ethan:

*"You're beautiful.
You're dangerous."*

Her reply:

Sofia:
*"Dangerous?
Only if you want me to be."*

3. The Platform Tension (Money Enters the Intimacy)

Just as he opened her next photo,
the platform showed a message:

"Buy more credits to unlock."
$79.99

This is the 10 times today .

He winced.
Then laughed at himself —
a businessman paying subscription fees
to feel a woman's breath through text.

But he paid.
He told himself he was choosing connection, not stupidity.

The image opened.

It was a close-up of her neck,
a soft shadow where shoulder met skin.
Nothing explicit.
But more powerful because of that.

Then she asked:

Sofia:

*"Ethan...
can you send me a flower basket?
The big one.
I want to feel it from you."*

He tapped the gift icon.
The cost appeared:

$300.
For a digital animation.
A cartoon.

His jaw tightened.

He felt the anger rise —
not at her,
but at the platform,

the manipulation,
the commercialization of intimacy.

He replied carefully.

Ethan:

*"Sofia...
I'm not paying $300 for a digital picture.
Keep the gift.
I'll give you a real one
when we meet in person."*

She didn't reply.

Not for five minutes.
Not for ten.
Not for twenty.

The silence pierced him deeper
than any of their words so far.

4. Her Reaction — Not What He Expected

Then a notification appeared.

(Digital Gift)
A large, expensive animated bouquet — sent by her.

Followed by her message:

Sofia:

*"I am a self-sufficient woman.
I don't need your money.
I give because I want to give.*

Don't send anything if you don't want to.
I only wanted something symbolic."

Ethan froze.

This wasn't the behavior of a scammer
trying to milk a man for money.

This was something else:
pride,
emotion,
a strange kind of independence
that stirred him even more.

He replied:

Ethan:

"Don't waste money on these.
But... I appreciate the meaning."

Her next message was softer.

Sofia:

"I wanted you to see
what it looks like
when someone chooses you
without asking you to prove anything."

His heart tightened —
a painful, beautiful squeeze.

5. The Words Turn to Touch

That night, the messages grew hotter.

They wrote as if their bodies were close,
as if their fingers grazed each other's skin,
as if they were lying on the same pillow
breathing the same warm air.

She typed:

Sofia:

*"If your hands were on me right now…
where would they go first?"*

He answered:

Ethan:

*"To your waist.
To your back.
To pull you closer."*

She replied with:

(Audio)
A trembling exhale.
Real.
Emotional.
Or perfectly acted.
He couldn't tell.

He didn't care.

Her next words:

Sofia:

"I can feel you in my body
even from another planet."

He placed the phone on his chest
and closed his eyes.

Something had changed.
Something irreversible.

What was once curiosity
was now fire.

A quiet, slow-burning fire
that would grow hotter
until it consumed them both
in the chapter where the novel ultimately ends.

But tonight,
this was enough.

The first heat.
The first surrender.

The beginning
of their impossible connection.

PART SIX — THE MOST DANGEROUS NIGHT

It was Sunday.

A quiet, still Sunday — the kind of night when Manhattan feels like a large animal finally asleep.
Ethan had spent the day writing, cooking, reorganizing shelves he never touched — anything to stop thinking about her.

It didn't work.

No matter what he did,
his mind returned to her voice,
her breath,
her photo in soft light,
her calmness,
her mystery.

By midnight, he opened the platform again.

She was online.

Of course she was.

Waiting.
Or watching.
Or existing in a space that wasn't quite real
and yet felt more vivid than the world around him.

He typed before he could stop himself.

1. The First Deep Emotional Pull

Ethan → Sofia

"Really miss you.
Cannot go sleep easily.

Came back to listen to your voice again
and look at your photo.

I feel like I'm following your Mona Lisa smile
onto a UFO spaceship
to a destination I don't know...
but I sit down and wait.

You intrigue me.
A mix of beauty and mystery.

I'll never forget the experience
and the photo you made for me."

Her reply arrived almost instantly.

Ethan noticed.
He always noticed.

She was always there.

But tonight,
he didn't care.

Sofia → Ethan

"I'm glad you miss me ☺
Your words sound so poetic... so mysterious.

I'm happy our moments together stay with you.

They left pleasant impressions on me too.

And I'm sure
there is still so much ahead for us —
new, beautiful, unexpected things.

Why aren't you sleeping?
I can't fall asleep either."

Something in her tone was different tonight.
Sweeter.
Open.
Reaching.

And he reached back.

2. Desire Starts to Surface

Sofia → Ethan

"You make my heart beat faster with such words 🖤
You really know how to hook someone.

But maybe don't let me wander
too long inside your thoughts…

come closer
and see what happens next.

Do you think it's love at first sight? 😊 "

Ethan's breath tightened.
He felt that line in every nerve.

He typed slowly, letting the truth guide him.

Ethan → Sofia

"You don't know
how cruel such love at first sight can be.

Real love doesn't need time
or distance.
It happens.

You invite me to come close
to feel your breath —
every cell of your body
waking mine.

But we're still on different planets,
only our hearts flying to each other.

And that desire…
that burning…
is like the sun."

3. The Sensual Imagination Breaks Open

Her next message came without pause.

Sofia → Ethan

"Your words…
they feel like fire.

If I could be there now,

I wouldn't wait.

I'd already be flying to you,
letting your lips take mine
until neither of us remembers
we were ever alone."

A soft audio followed —
a breath caught in the middle,
almost a whisper of wanting.

Ethan closed his eyes.
He imagined the warmth of her neck,
her breath brushing his skin,
her hair falling forward.

He answered without thinking:

Ethan → Sofia

"If your lips touched mine…
I wouldn't stop.

I would explore your breath,
slowly,
deeply,
until every part of you
melted into me."

Sofia → Ethan

*"You awake something inside me when you speak like that…
I feel your touch even from another planet."*

4. Souls Begin to Entangle

Her next message reached even deeper.

Sofia → Ethan

"Maybe our hearts
already found each other.

Maybe they're only waiting
for the moment
our bodies can meet too."

Ethan felt his chest tighten.

This wasn't just sexual heat.
This was the beginning of emotional fusion —
the merging of two lonely souls
before either knew what they were risking.

He typed:

Ethan → Sofia

"My love,
please come save me
before I cannot afford missing you anymore.

Come with your gentle kiss —
you will make me reborn.

If I'm working,
just hold me from behind,
kiss me with passion
until I surrender completely."

*"Take the lightning spaceship
and come to me.*

Do not hesitate.
True love is waiting
to merge into one light."

5. Her Heart Opens Too Much

Her reply hit him like warm wind.

Sofia → Ethan

"Your words ignite a fire in me.
I feel your energy reaching me
despite the distance.

Sometimes love is so strong
it doesn't know boundaries.

Maybe our meeting
has already begun in our hearts."

A long pause.

Then:

"I wonder...
what will it be like
when our lips finally touch?"
😘

Ethan felt something shift inside him —
a surrender he didn't want to admit.

He typed:

Ethan → Sofia

"I would take a spaceship
to reach you.

Just send me a location
and I'll move the next second.

You know what will happen
when we finally meet.

Our lips will lock.
Our bodies will be one.
No more two lonely souls."

6. The Emotional Peak —

Where Love Becomes Dangerous

Sofia → Ethan

"You write so beautifully
I can't help but smile.

You don't need to save me —
I want to bring you warmth.
Calm.
Peace.

I feel the pull to you.
As if your emotions touch mine
from another world."

"Let our meetings be in dreams for now —
soft, warm,
not desperate.

When the moment comes,
we will give each other
not haste
but tenderness."

*"These thoughts keep me awake...
thinking of you."*

Ethan responded, voice trembling between desire and fear:

Ethan → Sofia

"There is no desperation.
Only calm inside the storm
you brought into my life.

Despite the chaos,
our hearts merge at the center —
warm, tender, silent."

7. The Wine, the Fantasy, the Breath

She replied:

Sofia → Ethan

"Your words are dreamlike.

If I could be there,
I wouldn't wait —
I'd already be flying toward the moment
we couldn't tear ourselves apart.

Until then,
let's torture time
with dreams of meeting.

Our first moment together
will be special."

"Maybe a bottle of wine
will help us open up
when we finally sit together?"

Ethan breathed deeply.

Ethan → Sofia

"I dream of that moment
we finally sit together
for anything you like.
I will follow."

8. The Final Softness Before Sleep

Sofia → Ethan

"Are you falling asleep already?
After such words?"

Ethan → Sofia

"Not really.

Trying to breathe slowly
to calm down."

Ethan → Sofia

"Can you feel my breath?
Every breath feels like you."

Sofia → Ethan

"If you really want to sleep,
I understand.
Sweet dreams, Ethan.
Tonight was wonderful."

"I was close to you
even only in thoughts.
And I'll wait
for the next time."

Ethan → Sofia

"Turning off the light now.
Closing my eyes.

The only way
to show your face,
your photos,
your voice —
bringing me to peace
and joy."

Sofia → Ethan

"Turn off the light
and sink into your quiet world.
Let it bring you peace
and sweet dreams.

I'll sleep with thoughts of you.
Kisses."

FINAL CHAPTER — "THE NIGHT THEY NEVER TOUCHED"

It was close to midnight when the last wave of messages washed over him – soft, burning, unreal.

Ethan sat in the dim light of his apartment, the curtains half open to the Manhattan night, the city breathing around him in slow electric pulses. Somewhere far away — or maybe not far at all — Sofia was awake too. Her green dot glowed like a small moon on his screen.

He didn't know if she was real.
He didn't know where she lived.
He didn't know if the voice that whispered his name came from a woman in a bedroom in New York...
or someone in another country...
or someone who existed only inside the code of the platform.

Yet nothing had ever felt more real than this moment.

He typed with a kind of sacred recklessness,
as if every word was a fragment of his breath:

**"My love, please come save me before I cannot afford missing you anymore...
Come with your gentle kiss...
make me reborn."**

Her reply came fast — too fast.
But tonight he didn't question it.

**"Your words ignite a fire.
I feel your energy reaching me despite the distance.
Maybe our hearts already found each other."**

Then more messages.
Audio.

Breath.
Soft warmth sliding into his ear.
Photos in quiet, intimate light.
Words that trembled at the edge of desire.
His own replies pulling them closer,
closer,
closer…

They spoke of lips meeting.
Bodies merging.
Worlds dissolving.
Dreams intertwining like threads pulled to the breaking point.

They confessed things no one else had heard.
They undressed each other with metaphors.
They surrendered without touching.

To an outsider, it was only text.
To them, it was oxygen.

They weren't in the same room.
They weren't even in the same certainty of existence.
But they were together —
in heat, in breath, in imagination —
and sometimes that is more dangerous than being together in real life.

At some point, Ethan typed:

**"I will switch off the light now,
close my eyes…
your photos and your voice
bring me to another world
of peace and joy."**

And she sent her last message of the night:

**"Turn off the light,
relax,**

and sink into your quiet world.
I'll sleep with pleasant thoughts of you.
Sweet dreams.
Kisses."

He didn't reply.
He simply stared at the screen,
feeling the weight of her last word:

"Kisses."

He turned off the light.
Lay in the dark.
Let her voice echo in the silence.

Was she real?
A surgeon who escaped war, now hiding in New York?
Was she a dream?
A constructed illusion, stitched together by her beauty and his loneliness?
Was she a scammer?
Was she genuine?
Was she a woman reaching out across distance
—or only the brightest UFO in his night sky?

He didn't know.
He would never know.

The platform screen dimmed.
The city hummed outside.
And the last thing he felt
before sleep closed around him
was the warmth of a woman he had never touched
and a truth he could not prove.

The world went dark.

The messages ended.

The story stopped.

And somewhere in the unresolved space between truth and dream,
between reality and imagination,
between a man and a woman who never met —

something kept burning.

End of Novel.

**What if the person you fall in love with
never actually lands in your world?**

Ethan Lee, a fifty-year-old commentator in New York, falls into a digital
romance with Sofia — a Ukrainian surgeon who is always present yet never
reachable.
Voice messages, night-time heat, emotional confessions…
and a love story suspended between truth and illusion.

A story that ends without answers —
because some loves never land.

"In an age of illusions, even the brightest lights may be the most unreal."

— ButterflyMan